Daniel's Winter Adventure

Adapted by Becky Friedman
Based on the screenplay "Daniel's Winter Adventure"
written by Jill Cozza Turner
Poses and layouts by Jason Fruchter

Simon Spotlight
New York London Toronto Sydney New Delhi

0 0022 0470504 6

SIMON SPOTLIGHT
An imprint of Simon & Schuster Children's Publishing Division
1230 Avenue of the Americas, New York, New York 10020
This Simon Spotlight paperback edition September 2016
© 2016 The Fred Rogers Company
All rights reserved, including the right of reproduction in whole or in part in any form.
SIMON SPOTLIGHT and colophon are registered trademarks of Simon & Schuster, Inc.
For information about special discounts for bulk purchases, please contact Simon & Schuster
Special Sales at 1-866-506-1949 or business@simonandschuster.com.
Manufactured in the United States of America 0816 LAK
10 9 8 7 6 5 4 3 2 1
ISBN 978-1-4814-6741-4
ISBN 978-1-4814-6742-1 (eBook)

It was a snowy day in the neighborhood, and Daniel and Prince Wednesday were playing outside.

"Snowball catch!" said Daniel, as he tossed a snowball to Prince Wednesday.

"Got it!" said Prince Wednesday, giggling as the snowball landed on his head. "Sort of."

Just then Daniel's dad came over, holding ice skates and pulling Daniel's sled behind him.

"Hi, boys!" said Dad. "The pond is frozen and safe for ice skating. Are you two ready to go?"

"Yes!" said Daniel and Prince Wednesday.

"Okay, hop on the sled," said Dad. "Next stop, the ice skating pond!"

"Yay!" cheered Daniel and Prince Wednesday.

Daniel, Dad, and Prince Wednesday sang as they made their way through the snow-covered neighborhood.

"We're going to the pond today to slide and glide and skate!
Won't you sled along with me? Sled along!
Won't you sled along with me?"

"Look! I see the skating pond!" said Daniel.

"That's right. It's just down that hill," said Dad.

"That *BIG* hill?" asked Daniel.

"That royally big hill?" added Prince Wednesday.

"I—I don't think I can sled down that hill," said Daniel. "What if we go too fast? Or tip over? I can't do it. It's too hard."

"If something seems hard to do, try it a little bit at a time," sang Dad.

"But how do we sled down a big hill a little bit at a time?" asked Daniel.

"If we walk down the hill, closer to the bottom, you can sled down a little bit of the big hill," said Dad.

Together they walked down the hill. "Hey!" Daniel said. "From down here it doesn't look so hard! I think I can do it."

So they sledded down a little bit of the hill, and it wasn't hard at all—it was fun!

“Hmm,” Daniel began, looking back at the sledding hill. “Maybe we could go a bit higher?”

“A royal yes!” exclaimed Prince Wednesday.

They sledded down the hill from a little higher up, and it was even more fun!

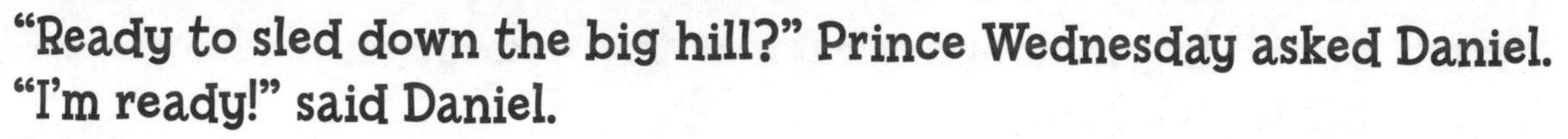

"Ready to sled down the big hill?" Prince Wednesday asked Daniel.
"I'm ready!" said Daniel.
"One . . . two . . . three . . . GO!" Daniel and Prince Wednesday shouted.

“Wheeeeeeeeeeeeee!”

Daniel loved sledding down the big hill so much that he imagined he was on a superfast racing sled.

When Daniel, Dad, and Prince Wednesday arrived at the skating pond, they saw Miss Elaina and her mom, Lady Elaine.

"Look!" said Daniel, "It's Miss Elaina . . . and she's ice-skating!"

"Hi, Dani—*OOF!*" said Miss Elaina, as she fell down.
"Are you okay?" asked Daniel.
"I'm okay," said Miss Elaina. "Ice-skating is just a little . . . whoa—oh—oh—slippery! But I like it."
"It looks . . . hard," said Daniel softly.

Dad called Daniel over to a bench to put on his ice skates.

"Dad?" said Daniel, "I'm not sure I want to go ice-skating anymore. It looks so slippery. . . . What if I fall?"

"Daniel," said Dad, "do you remember what to do when something seems hard?"

Daniel nodded. "*If something seems hard to do*—like ice-skating—*try it a little bit at a time.*"

Dad helped Daniel try skating a little bit at a time.

First Daniel took Dad's hands . . .

then he bent his knees and looked straight ahead . . .

and marched his feet:
March! March! March!

Until finally:
"I'm skating! I'm skating!"
said Daniel, happily.

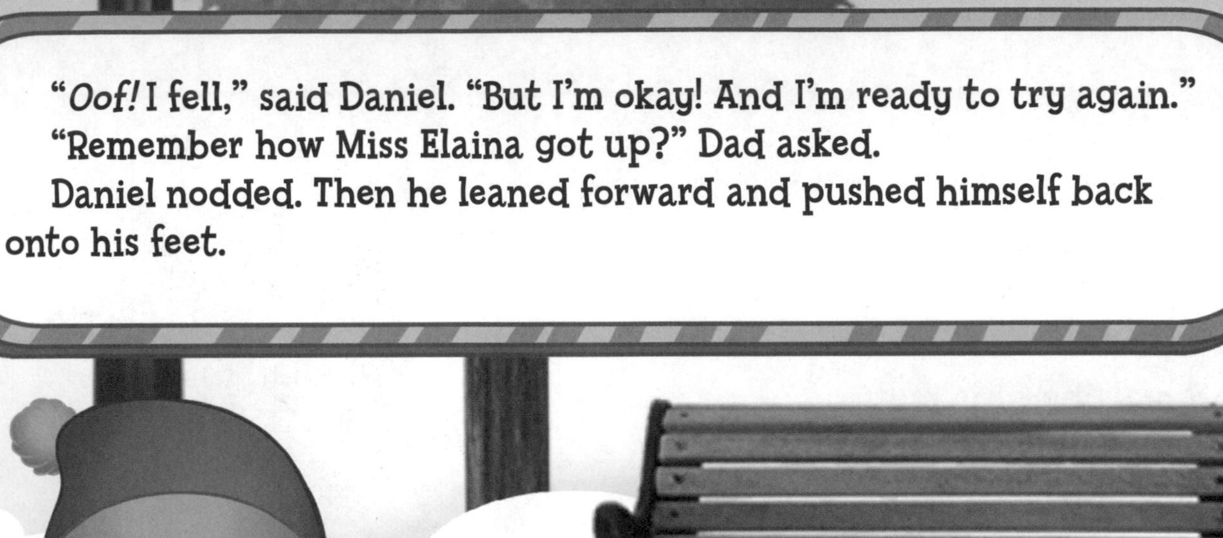

"*Oof!* I fell," said Daniel. "But I'm okay! And I'm ready to try again."

"Remember how Miss Elaina got up?" Dad asked.

Daniel nodded. Then he leaned forward and pushed himself back onto his feet.

Just as Daniel skated back to the bench, Mom Tiger arrived at the pond with Daniel's baby sister, Margaret.

"Dan-dan!" said Margaret, as she stepped one foot toward Daniel.

"Look, Daniel!" Mom said. "I think Margaret wants to try to walk for the first time!"

"Come on, Margaret! You can do it!" said Daniel. "Just try it a little bit at a time."

Margaret took one step . . . and another . . . and another . . . until she walked all the way over to Daniel!

"Margaret, you did it!" cheered Daniel. "You walked! I tried something new today, and you did too."

"You are a great big brother and a big helper," Mom said, smiling.

Daniel and his friends spent the rest of the afternoon skating and falling down and getting back up again . . . and having a lot of fun.

I didn't think I could ice-skate, but then I did it, a little bit at a time. Even though it was hard, it was grr-ific! Is there something new that you would like to try? Just remember, *if something seems hard to do, try it a little bit at a time.* Ugga Mugga!